THE BIRD TALISMAN

THE BIRD TALISMAN

AN EASTERN TALE

by

HENRY ALLEN WEDGWOOD

illustrated by

GWEN RAVERAT

FABER AND FABER LIMITED
24 Russell Square
London

Published in October mcmxxxix
by Faber & Faber Limited
24 Russell Square London W.C.1
Reprinted mcmxlvii
Second edition mcmlxiv
Reprinted mcmlxv
Printed in Great Britain
by John Dickens & Co Ltd Northampton

The following Fairy Tale was written by my great-uncle Harry Wedgwood, for his children. It was printed in *The Family Tutor* in 1852; and it was so much liked by all the children of the Wedgwood and Darwin families that in 1887 his sister, Mrs Darwin, had it privately printed for the next generation, in the form of a small book. Henry Allen Wedgwood was a grandson of Josiah Wedgwood of Etruria, the potter; he was born in 1799; became a barrister, and married his cousin Jessie Wedgwood, also a grandchild of Josiah. He died in 1885, so that I never knew him, but I have always heard that he was a genial and charming man and that he was held to be the wit of the family. He made some amusing pen-and-ink drawings to illustrate this story; but they were very few and very small, and we children always felt that the appearance of the book was rather arid; so that I have at last overcome my feeling of sacrilege in tampering with a sacred work and have tried to illustrate it myself. And, in spite of the very kind approbation of Uncle Harry's surviving grandchildren, I feel I ought to apologize to all my relations, both known and unknown, for the presumption of the attempt. I should add, that the author was never in the East in his life; and that neither he nor I have made any effort to be accurately Indian.

G. RAVERAT

THE BIRD TALISMAN

CHAPTER I

THERE was once an old hermit, who lived in a hut near the source of the Ganges. He was very kind to all birds and beasts; and they were so accustomed to him that the very wild beasts were neither afraid of him nor would hurt him. One day, as he sat by the stream watching two daws that were flying about and playing together in the air, one of the birds happened to fall into the water, which was very rapid, and was swept away by the stream, and would have been drowned if the old hermit had not run to its help, and, stepping into the water, pulled out the daw with his hooked staff.

He laid the bird in the sun, and as soon as it was dry the two daws both flew away to a high rock, just above where the Ganges rises. The hermit saw them fly into a little cave, halfway up the rock, and presently come out again, and fly back towards him; they alighted close to him, and one of them laid a ring down at his feet. He picked it up and put it on his finger, and he was immediately astonished to hear the daw speak to him and say, "Good hermit, please to accept this ring, for having saved my life, and for your kindness to all poor birds and beasts; it is a magic ring, and

whoever wears it can understand the language of birds, and all birds will do whatever he orders them when he shows them the ring. Can we do anything to serve you?"

The hermit answered, "Yes; I was formerly king of Cashmere, and was dethroned by my son-in-law, and obliged to conceal myself in this disguise. I should like, before I die, to hear some news of the queen—my daughter, and of my former kingdom; and if you can fly over the mountains to Cashmere, and bring me back some news, I shall be for ever thankful."

Away flew the two daws, and were out of sight in a moment, and for some days the hermit saw no more of them; but one evening, as he sat at the door of his hut, he saw two black specks in the sky, which, as they came nearer, turned out to be the two daws. They perched on the bench by his side, and one of them said, "We have brought you sorrowful

news from Cashmere. The queen, your daughter, is dead, leaving one little daughter; and the king is married again; and, from what we heard from the parrot that belonged to the late queen, the present queen is very unkind to her step-daughter; and there is reason to fear that as soon as the king leaves his capital to go and hunt in the mountains, the wicked queen will take the opportunity to kill your little granddaughter, or get rid of her in some way."

The old hermit was very much grieved at this account, and could not sleep all night for thinking about it. In the morning the two daws came, as usual, to fly about the banks of the stream; as soon as he saw them he beckoned to them, and they flew to him. "Take this ring," said he, drawing the magic ring from his finger, "and carry it to my granddaughter, and tell her, when she wants help or advice, to call to any bird she sees, and they will, no doubt, advise her and help her; it is the only help I can give her."

"We will go to her," replied the daws, "and give her the ring; and we will stay with her, and do all we can for her, and, if possible, we will bring her to you."

Away flew the two birds with the ring, over the tops of the mountains, and across the plains, till they came to the palace of the king of Cashmere. They flew straight to the chamber of the little princess, whom they found feeding her parrot; they laid down the ring before her, and she put it on her finger, and was immediately able to understand what the birds said, and to hold conversation with them.

The two daws told the little princess all that the old hermit had told them, and the parrot told her all that had happened when her grandfather lost the kingdom. The poor little princess cried very much, and said she should be very glad to go to her grandfather, "for," said she, "the queen is so unkind to me, and never lets me see my father without being present, so that I dare not complain to him; and the queen sets everybody against me, and nobody loves me, or cares for me, except my dear old parrot."

"My dear child," replied the parrot, stooping down from her perch to give her a kiss with her great horny bill—"you may always depend on my loving you as if you were my own child and I had hatched you myself—for I was here when you were born and your poor mother before you. As for what these worthy birds say about taking you to your grandfather, it will be a difficult and dangerous undertaking; but after the king goes on his hunting expedition to the mountains, it will not be safe for my dear child to remain here in the power of that wicked queen."

It was then settled that the two daws should roost in the palace garden, and should be always within call in case they should be wanted; and the old parrot promised to keep a good watch in the palace and find out whether the queen was planning any mischief against the princess.

CHAPTER II

Soon after this the king set off on his grand hunting expedition to the mountains; and the very next day the two daws brought word to the parrot that the queen's favourite slave, Baboof, was busy gathering plants in the garden, and that they had seen him gather some hemlock, some henbane, some opium poppies, and several other poisonous plants. As soon as the parrot heard this she flew out of the window, and having seen what Baboof was doing, flew straight to the queen's apartment, where she concealed herself, to watch the queen's proceedings.

Presently Baboof brought in his bundle of poisonous herbs, and the queen chopped them up, and set them to boil in a pot, on a pan of charcoal that was burning in the chimney. She then took some flour and sweetmeats out of a box, and made a cake and kneaded it up with the liquor from the poisonous herbs in the pot. She then set the cake to bake on the charcoal, and the parrot stole away without being perceived, and flew to the princess's apartment, where she found the two daws.

"There is no time to be lost," cried she; "if the princess stays here any longer she will be poisoned. The queen is at this moment baking a poisoned cake for her. Come, my dear child, let us escape at once."

The princess immediately rose in great alarm, and ran to the door, the three birds following her; but the door was locked. The window was too high above the ground for the princess to get out of it, and, besides, there was a sentinel in the garden just opposite the window. Before they could determine what to do, the queen came, and unlocking the door, entered the room with a nice-looking cake in a dish. She did not see the two daws, because they flew out of the window as the queen came in at the door.

"Here is a cake for you, my dear," said the queen, "which I have made with my own hands"; and so saying she put it on the table and went out, locking the door after her.

As soon as she was gone, the parrot called the two daws and told them to take the cake and throw it over the garden-wall into the lake, which they did, and then came back.

The princess remained locked up all that day, and her usual meal was not brought to her; but the two daws gathered some figs for her in the garden, and she and her three birds made a very good supper of them. In the morning the queen came to see whether the princess was dead, and when she saw her still alive she was furious, and seizing her by the hair, began to beat her, and tried to get her hands round her neck to strangle her. In the meantime, the parrot flew out of the window straight to the queen's nursery, where the queen's little baby was in his cradle. The parrot picked up a lighted stick from a fire that was burning on the hearth, and set fire to the window-curtains, and then flew along the passages leading to the princess's apartment, screaming, "Fire!—Fire! The nursery is on fire!—the little prince will be burnt to death!"

And all the slaves in the palace began to cry, "Fire!—Fire!"

All this did not take two minutes; and the queen had not been able to strangle the princess, when she heard the outcry, and immediately leaving the princess lying on the floor, ran to the nursery to save her own child.

The little princess rose from the ground as well as she was able; and the parrot screaming to her that now was the time to escape, she ran out of the door and downstairs into the garden, where she was joined by the two daws, and the old parrot scuffled along before them and led the way to a little door in the wall. The princess with some difficulty drew back the bolt and opened the door; and going through this, they found themselves on the shore of the lake. There were two swans floating near the shore, and the parrot told the little princess to show them the ring and order them to take her to the other side of the lake. As soon as the swans saw the ring which the princess held up to them, they swam towards her, bowing their heads and asking what she wished them to do.

"Take me across the lake," said she.

They immediately placed themselves side by side, and the princess, wading into the water, placed herself between them, with one arm over each of their backs; and so supporting herself, almost up to the shoulders in the water, she floated between the swans, and they carried her safely over to the other side with the parrot sitting quite dry and comfortable on her shoulder, and the two daws flying overhead.

When they reached the other side, the princess landed, and the swans took leave of her, and swam back again. The princess found a retired place amongst the rocks, and taking off her clothes, spread them to dry in the sun; and the parrot told one of the daws to sit on the top of the rock and keep watch, while the other flew back at the princess's desire to see what had become of the queen's baby and the nursery that was set on fire.

By the time the clothes were dry the daw came back, and told the princess that no harm had happened to the child, and that the fire was extinguished. He also said that the palace was in great confusion; Baboof and all the slaves running about everywhere looking for the princess, and that a reward of fifty pieces of gold was offered to whoever would bring her to the queen.

The parrot begged the princess to put on her clothes and follow her, for that they had a long way to go before they should be safe from their pursuers. So they all set out; the daws flying high in the air and keeping a good look-out on every side, and the old parrot leading the way before the princess over the rocks. They soon reached a large wood; and while one of the daws flew high over the trees on the look-out, the other came down into the wood, and flew along the pathway in advance of the princess. They met several people in the wood; but the daw in advance always called out in the birds' language, and the princess hid herself in the bushes till the persons they met passed by. Nobody took any notice of the birds.

So they travelled on till the princess was quite tired out and hungry. The parrot then called down the daw that was flying overhead, and asked him whether he had seen any signs of water; and he said there was a little cascade falling from a rock not far to the right. The parrot told the two daws to see if they could find any fruit in the wood, and to bring it to the princess at the cascade; and then persuaded the princess to rise and follow her, tired as she was. They soon heard the noise of the waterfall, and, guided by the sound, made their way to the foot of a rock, down which the water fell into a rocky and deep bason; here the princess drank her fill, and so did the parrot; and then they sat down on the grass to wait for the daws, who soon made their appearance with as many figs and grapes as they could carry. These were soon eaten by the princess and the parrot, and, as the daws had found them at no great distance, they were not long in bringing a fresh supply, and they all made a very hearty meal.

The place was so pleasant and so retired, that they determined to rest there till the next day; and the birds busied themselves in collecting dry leaves and grass to make a bed for the princess, who soon learnt to make herself useful, too; and before night they had all collected a very comfortable heap of litter under a brow of the rock which kept off the falling dew. On this heap the princess lay down, and was soon fast asleep. The three birds went to roost in a tree close by, and took it in turns to keep watch all night.

CHAPTER III

In the morning, the whole party breakfasted on figs and grapes, and resumed their journey in the same order as the day before. Towards noon, and when they had been travelling on in silence for some time, the daw in advance saw a man coming to meet them, and immediately called out to warn the princess. She heard the cry of the daw, but could not understand what he said, but seeing him come flying back, and making a loud cawing, she thought something was wrong, and hid herself in the bushes till the man was past; she then rejoined the birds, but found she could not understand a word they said; at last she perceived that she had lost her magic ring, which being too large for her slender finger, had slipped off, unperceived, in the course of the morning's walk; she held up her hands to show the parrot that the ring was gone; and great was the grief of all—the little girl crying, the parrot screaming, and the two daws cawing in mournful concert. At last the parrot made signs to the princess to follow her, and they all turned back the way they came, carefully looking for the lost ring, but in vain; for they reached the cascade without seeing anything of the ring.

It was now evening, and the daws having gathered some figs and grapes for supper, the little princess lay down to sleep on her bed of the night before. She felt very unhappy at being no longer able to converse with her dear birds, but she soon cried herself to sleep. In the morning they all set out again to search for the ring. While they were thus employed, the two daws came suddenly upon a soldier lying under a tree.

"Here is a man!"—cried one—"fly back and warn the princess!"

"Who goes there?" cried the soldier, jumping up; and as he rose, the daws saw the lost ring glittering on his finger. Immediately the charm worked, and the daws were obliged to answer the soldier's question.

"We are two unfortunate daws, at your service," said they.

The soldier was astonished to hear the birds talk, and exclaimed—"How is this? How can birds like you talk?"

"Sir," replied one of them, "you have a magic ring on your finger, which enables you to understand what we say, and compels us to answer your questions."

"Does it?" said the soldier, "then tell me what princess

you were talking of, just now?" "The princess of Cashmere," answered the daw.

"Why there is a reward of fifty pieces of gold for whoever finds her!" said the soldier—"Is she anywhere hereabouts?"

The poor daws were very unwilling to betray the princess, but they could not resist the magic of the ring; so they were forced to confess that the princess was close at hand, and the soldier immediately proceeded to look for, and soon found her. He seized her by the arm, and, in

spite of her tears and cries, dragged her along the path, the three birds following with many doleful cries. By and by they reached the shore of the lake, where they found a boat moored. Into this the princess was forced to go, and the soldier getting in himself, the parrot managed to scramble in, and hid herself under one of the seats. The soldier rowed the boat across the lake, and the daws flew overhead. They landed near the postern door of the palace, and knocking at the door, it was opened by Baboof, who grinned horribly when he saw the princess, and led them immediately to the queen's apartment, while the three birds concealed themselves in the garden.

The queen gave the soldier the promised reward, and ordered Baboof to lock the princess up in her own room, and to set guards opposite both the door and the windows to prevent her escaping again. She then inquired of the soldier how he had found the princess; and he told her how he had found a magic ring in the wood, which enabled him to understand the language of birds; and how he had learnt from the daws where the princess was. As soon as the queen heard of the magic ring, she offered the soldier fifty more pieces of gold for it, which he gladly accepted, and went his way.

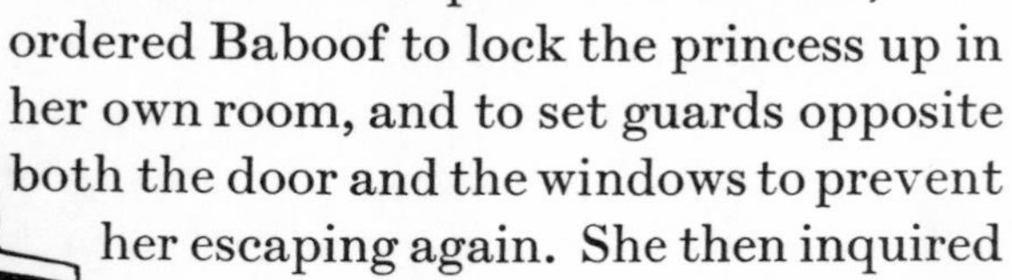

The queen was delighted at getting possession of the magic ring—for she had often heard of it in her youth, and knew that it formerly belonged to the famous enchanter, Moozuffer, and that, at his death, it had been carried away by the birds, and concealed, that no other person might rule them as Moozuffer had ruled them in his lifetime, by means of this ring. Looking out of the window, she saw the two daws sitting mournfully on a tree in the garden, and holding up the ring to them, called them to her, and ordered them to go to the forest on the other side of the lake, in the midst of which they would find an immense rock, with perpendicular sides. At the foot of this rock they would find a pomegranate-tree growing, in the trunk of which was inclosed a living toad. She told the daws to bring her one of the pomegranates from this tree; and she told them, also, to swallow a pomegranate seed each, for the seeds of that pomegranate were an antidote to every poison, and unless they swallowed one, they would perish in the next service she required of them, which was to fly up to the top of the rock, and bring her a piece of the gum of a poisonous tree which grew there.

The two daws flew away to the forest, and soon found the pomegranate-tree growing at the foot of the rock. They tapped at the trunk with their bills, and listened, and heard the toad croak inside the tree. They then swallowed some of the seeds that lay scattered under the tree, and having gathered each a pomegranate, they flew to the top of the rock, which they found quite bare of all plants, or living things, and scattered over with the skeletons of birds, which had been poisoned by the smell of the poison-tree, in flying over the rock. On the highest point of the rock grew one small, stunted tree, from the bark of which dropped a black-looking gum. One of the daws picked up a piece of this gum, and then they both flew back to the palace, carrying the gum and the two pomegranates. One of the pomegranates they dropped amongst a thicket of bushes in the garden, and the other they carried, together with the gum, to the queen, who immediately swallowed one of the pomegranate-seeds herself, and gave another to Baboof, who was with her, to prevent being poisoned by the smell of the gum, which she then put into a golden box, and sealed it up.

As soon as the daws left the queen, they flew straight to the little princess's window, where they found the parrot. They told her what they had done about the poisonous gum and the pomegranates, and they all agreed that a new attempt would be made to poison the princess; and to be prepared for this, the daws went and fetched the pomegranate which they had dropped in the garden. The parrot pecked a hole in it, and ate one of the seeds herself, and then carried the pomegranate to the princess, who was sitting crying in a corner, and made signs to her to eat one of the seeds. The princess did not like to do this, for the pomegranate was exactly of the colour of the skin of a toad, and did not look at all tempting; but the parrot made so many signs, and coaxed the princess so, that she at last swallowed one of the seeds, and the parrot hid the pomegranate under the bed. She had hardly done so, and, hearing the key turned in the door, concealed herself also, when Baboof entered, with a loaf of bread and a jar of water, which he put on a table, and went out. As soon as he was gone, the parrot came from under the bed. The princess was very hungry and thirsty, but was afraid to eat or drink, though the parrot, knowing that the pomegranate-seed was an antidote to the poison, did all she could by signs to encourage the princess to eat.

While the parrot was making a great fuss, pecking the bread, and sipping the water, and making all sorts of impatient noises, the two daws flew in at the window, with the magic ring in one of their bills. As soon as the princess touched the ring, she immediately understood what the birds said, and they told her how they had recovered the ring—that when Baboof came in with the loaf, they had flown out of the window, and perching in a tree opposite the queen's window, they had seen the queen sitting there, playing with her little boy, who pulled the ring off her finger, and rolled it along the window-seat, and at last let it fall out of the window; that the queen immediately left the window, to send one of her slaves to pick up the ring; but before she could do so, and without being seen by any one, the daws picked it up, and brought it to the princess. Great was her joy at being again able to talk with her birds, and when they had told her all about the poisonous gum, and the antidote, she was no longer afraid to eat the bread, and drink the water, and after making a hearty supper she went to bed.

CHAPTER IV

In the morning, Baboof came to see whether the princess was dead, and was much surprised to find she was alive, though she had eaten so much of the poisoned bread. He said nothing, however, but went down to tell the queen, who was in the garden, looking again for the ring, under the window from which the baby had dropped it. The parrot told one of the daws to go and listen to what they said; and accordingly the daw went slily, and hid himself in a bush close to the queen, where he could hear all that passed. The queen was very much surprised at the princess escaping the effects of the poison, and said she must have some talisman, or charm, about her.

"However," said she, "to-night you shall take her to the balcony that looks on the lake, and throw her into the water with a stone round her neck; and in the morning we will pretend she has died in the night, and have a false funeral and a coffin filled with rubbish, which we will bury."

The daw flew back to tell this dreadful news to his companions, and they consulted together without telling the princess, for fear of frightening her; but when they had settled their plans, they then told her not to be alarmed, but to leave everything to them, and they would save her life.

There lived just outside the palace walls, in a hut on the shore of the lake, a poor fisherman, who used to spread his nets in the water, below the walls of the palace; and the little princess had often sat in the balcony with her attendants and watched him fishing, and often used to buy his fish of him and draw it up with a basket and string, and let down the money in the same way, so that she had made quite a friendship with the old man. The parrot used to be of these parties—for she was very fond of fish—and the old fisherman and she were on very good terms. To this old fisherman's hut the parrot and the two daws now flew, taking the ring with them, and putting it on the old man's finger, so that he could understand what she said, the parrot told him that his little patroness was in need of his assistance to save her life. The old man immediately said he would do anything for her, even at the risk of his own life. He was then told the whole state of affairs, and promised to obey all the parrot's orders.

The parrot and the old fisherman settled between them what was best to be done to save the princess. The old man said that he would lay his nets under the balcony, so as to catch the princess as soon as she should be thrown into the water; and that she might float on the surface instead of sinking, he hit on the following plan. He took a number of corks from an old net, and told the parrot and the two daws to fly with them, one by one, to the princess's room, and tell her to cut them into small pieces, and string them on a piece of twine, and wrap this round and round her body so as to form a sort of jacket, by means of which she would be able to float in the water, in spite of the weight of the stone that Baboof and the queen had talked of tying round her neck. But to make sure, the fisherman sent the princess a little sharp knife, by the parrot, and sent her word to keep it concealed under her sleeves, in order to cut away the stone from her neck.

When all this was prepared and settled, the parrot flew back with the ring and one of the corks to the princess, and the daws followed with as many pieces of cork as they could carry, and they all three flew backwards and forwards with the corks till they had brought as many as would be wanted. The little princess cut the corks in pieces, and strung them on a piece of strong twine which the fisherman sent her; and she obeyed the directions brought by the parrot—wrapping the corks round and round her body, and concealing them under her pelisse.

By the time this was done, it began to grow dark, and by and by Baboof made his appearance, and told the princess she must come with him. He led her by the hand through the garden, and up to the balcony overlooking the lake; and as they passed through the garden he picked up a large stone, and wrapped it in a handkerchief; and when they reached the balcony he suddenly tied the handkerchief round her neck, putting his hand on her mouth to prevent her crying out, and at the same time lifted her over the balustrade and threw her into the water. But she was prepared for this, and in an instant, as he was lifting her up, she cut the handkerchief with the knife, so that the stone fell into the water at the same time with herself, and sank to the bottom, while she floated by means of her cork jacket. It was quite dark, and Baboof hearing the splash, and then all being still, thought she had sunk to the bottom, and left the balcony to tell the queen what he had done.

In the meantime, the old fisherman was lying concealed with his boat under the projection of the balcony, and had

spread his net so that whatever fell from the balcony should be within it. As soon, therefore, as he heard the splash, he began quietly to draw in his net, and soon brought the floating princess to the side of his boat and lifted her in.

He then rowed quietly away to his own hut, and landed with the princess. He showed her into a little room, where a comfortable bed was prepared for her, and where she found the parrot and the two daws already arrived. They had accompanied the princess in the dark to the balcony, and when they had ascertained she was safe in the boat, they had flown on before to the fisherman's hut. The little princess went to bed immediately, for her clothes were all wet; and as soon as she was in bed the old man brought her a plate of bread and fish for her supper, after eating which, and giving some to her three birds, she fell asleep.

In the morning, the old man went a-fishing, leaving her locked up in the hut, and the two daws flew to the palace to get intelligence. They found everything in a bustle in the palace, with a grand funeral preparing, and looking in at the window of the princess's room, they saw a magnificent coffin lying on the bed, with wax tapers all round it, and the attendants in deep mourning. They flew back to the princess with this news, and the parrot said to her—"Now, my dear, you may rest here in peace till we can get an opportunity of escaping to your grandfather. The queen thinks you are drowned; and I am sure we may trust the old fisherman."

As she said this, the old man came in with a great basket of fish, of which he chose the nicest for the princess to eat, and took out the rest to sell in the city. With the money he got for the fish he bought food and other necessaries, and enough cloth to make the princess a complete suit of common clothes, which she cut out and made for herself.

The late queen had taught the little princess to work, and she soon made herself a very neat suit of clothes such as poor people's children wear; for the old fisherman and the parrot thought she would be safer in that disguise. They

also told her to keep in doors, for fear of being seen and known by anybody. There was, however, a little garden at the back of the fisherman's cottage, in which she was allowed to go; and she managed to pass her time pleasantly enough between doing the work of the house, mending the nets—which the fisherman taught her to do—and playing with her birds.

Every day the old man went a-fishing, and, with the money he got by selling his fish, he bought whatever was necessary for the little household, and everything prospered with them for a time. But the season for catching the best fish was nearly over, and by and by he was less successful in his fishing, and at last he had great difficulty in getting enough to eat. The fruit season was over, too, so that the daws were unable to find any fruit for their mistress, and the household began to be reduced to great distress.

One day the old man came home from fishing without having caught a single fish, and he was just sitting down with the little girl, to dine on a little bit of mouldy bread, which was all he had left in the house, when the two daws flew in at the window, with each of them a piece of gold money in their bills, which they laid on the table and then told the princess how they had got it. They said that they had been flying all about the palace garden, to see if they could find any fruit left, and had perched to rest themselves on the top of an old chimney. They peeped down the funnel, which was very wide and short, and saw something glittering at the bottom, and one of them flew down, and found himself in the royal treasury, with quantities of jewels and money scattered all about. He called to the other to come down, and they each picked up a piece of gold and flew up the chimney with them, and so home.

The old man was delighted at the sight of the gold, and said he considered it the princess's own money, for the king, if he knew it, would be glad to give her a thousand times as much if she wanted it; so he immediately went out and brought provisions, and whatever else was wanted. While the money lasted, they all lived as comfortably as possible; and when it was all spent, the daws went and got some more.

CHAPTER V

One day the little princess was playing by herself in the garden, and looking up, she saw a gipsy woman looking at her over the low wall of the garden. As soon as the woman saw that she was observed by the princess, she began to bow down her head, and kiss her hand to her very humbly, and said—"Oh, my sweet young lady!—give me a morsel of food, for I am starving to death." The princess ran to the house, and fetched her a piece of bread, and handed it to her over the wall, when the gipsy suddenly threw a cloak over the little girl's head, and wrapping it round her face, so that she could neither see nor cry out, she caught her by the arm, and pulled her over the wall. Then, folding the cloak close round her, she threw her like a bundle over her back, and ran off with her, threatening to cut her throat if she made any noise.

She was carried in this manner a long way and felt almost stifled by the cloak. When at last she was set down, and the cloak unwrapped from round her, she found herself in a wood, surrounded by a large family of gipsies, who had a fire of sticks burning on the ground, and two or three small tents pitched, and several asses grazing close by. The woman who had kidnapped her told her not to cry, and no harm should happen to her; that she should be taken to a grand city, and sold to some great prince or princess, and live in splendour and riches all her life; but if she tried to escape or give any alarm, she should be murdered.

As soon as the woman had concluded this speech, the gipsies took down their tents, and packed up everything, and loading their donkeys, set off without delay. The little princess was put on the back of one of the asses that carried the bedding, and in this manner she

rode very comfortably, but was much frightened and very unhappy. She looked all around in hopes of seeing her two daws, but they were not to be seen. She was afraid the gipsies would steal her ring; so she took an opportunity, when she was not observed, to slip it into the folds of her hair, under her turban, and fastened it there. They travelled in this way till some time after dark, when they halted in a retired wood, where they lighted a fire and pitched their tents. The gipsies sat down to a very good supper, of which the princess partook, and afterwards she slept in one of the tents.

The princess wakened very early in the morning, and seeing the gipsy-woman and children who slept in the tent with her fast asleep, and the door of the tent open, she stepped softly out, thinking to run away, but was stopped on the outside by a growl from a large dog, which lay a few yards from the tent door. She saw that if she attempted to escape, the dog would fly at her, or, at least, waken all the gipsies by his barking; so she stood quite still, and the dog lay quiet, only keeping his eyes fixed on her.

Just then, she heard a wood-pigeon cooing in a tree overhead, and looking up, she saw the bird perched on a bough just above her. She immediately drew the ring out of her hair, and held it up to the pigeon, making a sign to it to come down and perch on her arm, which it did. Then, for fear of wakening the gipsies, she whispered to the pigeon to fly to the old fisherman's hut, and tell the parrot and the daws what had become of her; and cutting off a lock of her hair, she told the pigeon to take it to the old fisherman as a token. Away flew the pigeon, and the princess returned into the tent, and lay down again, carefully hiding the ring in her hair as before.

By and by the gipsies got up, and prepared breakfast,

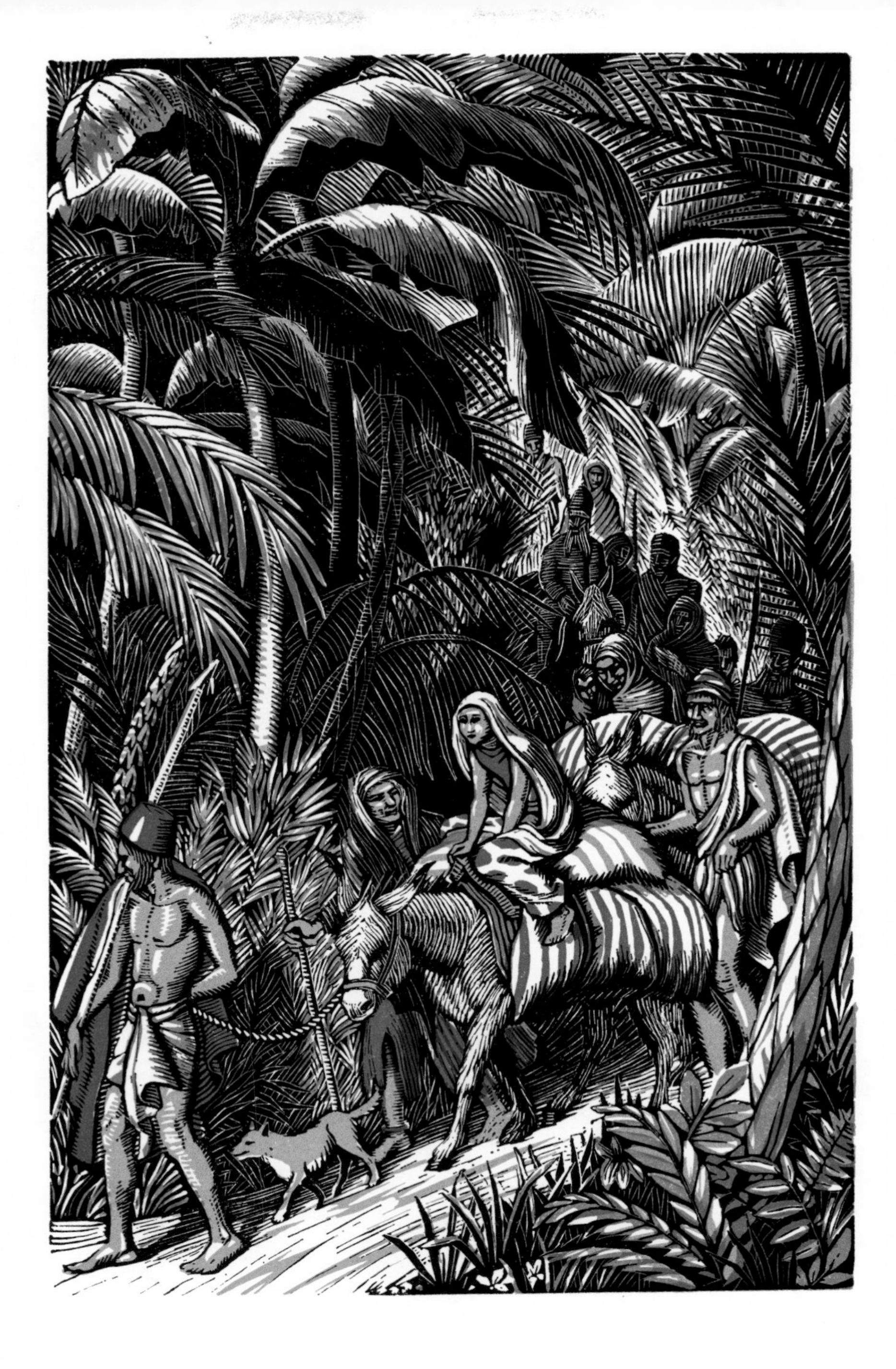

after which everything was packed up, and they resumed their journey, the princess sometimes walking with the gipsy children, and, when she was tired, riding on one of the asses. The gipsy woman who had stolen her often talked to her, and told her how well off she would be if she was bought as a slave by some great prince at Lahore, where they were going. So they journeyed all day, only stopping to dine and rest, during the hottest part of the afternoon, in a shady grove of trees.

A little before sunset they came to a wood, where there was a spring of water, and here they unloaded the asses, and made preparations for passing the night. The princess was allowed to walk about by herself, but the dog that had watched her in the morning was ordered by signs to go with her; and he seemed to understand very well that he was not to let her escape, for if ever she quickened her pace, or seemed to be going too far from the tents, the dog began to growl.

At last she sat down under a tree at the outskirts of the wood, and as she was looking towards the way they had come, she saw what seemed a strange looking bird flying towards her: as it came nearer, she saw it was not one bird, but three, all flying in a bunch together; and when they came still nearer, she saw that it was

her dear old parrot and the two daws. The two daws held the two ends of a stick in their claws, and the parrot held the middle of it in her beak, and by the support of the stick, and helping herself along by flapping her wings, she made a very good flight of it. As soon as they were within hearing, the little princess began to call out to them, and when the parrot heard her voice, she let go the stick and flew down to the princess, and, perching on her shoulder, kissed her over and over again. The two daws, too, dropped the stick and came down and perched on a bush out of the dog's reach, and told the princess how glad they were to see her again. They told her also how the wood-pigeon had brought news of what had become of her to the fisherman's hut, and that they had immediately set out after her, asking all the birds they met whether they had seen her, and so tracing her out without much difficulty. They said that the old fisherman seemed to understand they were gone to find her, and had received the lock of hair in token that she was alive and safe.

While she was thus eagerly talking with her birds, she did not perceive that two of the gipsy children who were a little older than herself had stolen after her behind the bushes, till they suddenly rushed out, and before the parrot could fly out of their way, they had caught her, and began to run back to the tents with their prize, crying out that

they had caught a parrot. The princess followed, crying, and begging them to give back her parrot, but they did not mind her. However, just as they came to the tents, and as the elder gipsies came out to see what was the matter, the parrot managed to bite their fingers, so that they let her go, and she flew up into a tree out of their reach.

The gipsy woman asked what was the matter, and the princess told her that the parrot was hers, and had found its way after her all the way from home, and that the other children had taken it from her; and she cried very much, and said the parrot was the only friend she had, and begged the woman to let her have it.

"Well," said the woman, "if you will be a good girl, and not make yourself unhappy, so that you may look well and fat when we come to sell you at Lahore, you shall keep your parrot."

She then ordered the other children not to meddle with the parrot, which then came down from its tree. As for the two daws, they kept always not far off in case of need.

Before going to bed that night, the gipsy woman brought some leaves out of the wood and boiled them in a pot, and with the liquor she washed the princess's face and arms and legs; and her skin turned as brown as that of the gipsies themselves.

"There, my dear," said the woman, "you will now pass for a gipsy; if people saw you with that pretty white skin of yours, they would guess you did not belong to us, and we should not be allowed to keep you."

When the princess was in bed the parrot roosted by her side, and before she went to sleep comforted her as well as she could, and told her that she need not be afraid of the gipsies, who would be sure to use her well that she might look well when she came to be sold, and so bring a good price.

And so it was; for the gipsies were very kind to her, and took great care of her. They travelled on many days, pitching their camp at night in quiet out of the way of public places. The princess often saw her two daws flying overhead, but she took no notice of them, for fear of being seen by the gipsies.

CHAPTER VI

One afternoon the whole party were sleeping in the shade, when the princess was awakened by the parrot pinching her ear with her bill. As soon as she opened her eyes, she saw the two daws fluttering and screaming amongst the branches of a thicket not far off, and crying out—"A tiger! a tiger! Awake! awake!"

"Wake the gipsies," cried the parrot, "or the tiger will be upon us."

The princess jumped up, and began screaming as loud as she could—"A tiger! a tiger! Awake! awake!" and the gipsies were soon awakened.

At this moment, the princess saw the eyes of the tiger glaring at her from under a bush, but, just as he was going to spring, one of the gipsies caught up a bundle of dry reeds, and lighting it at the fire where the pot was boiling, flung the reeds all in a blaze into the tiger's face, which so frightened him that he turned off with a loud roar, and bounding across the plain with great swiftness, was out of sight in a very few minutes.

The next day they left the wooded country and entered on the desert. They travelled all day without seeing a living creature or a living plant. It was one vast plain of dry sand,

"But do not fear," she said, "I will take care that you shall only be sold to a good mistress, who will bring you up well and make you happy."

A few days after this conversation, they came in sight of the towers and minarets of the great city of Lahore. They encamped in a grove not far from the gate of the city, and the gipsy woman having mixed with water some white powder which she took out of a little box, washed the princess with it, and her skin became as white as before it was dyed brown.

CHAPTER VII

The next morning the gipsy woman took the princess into the city with the parrot on her arm, and after going through a great many streets, they reached a bazaar where was the slave-market. The slaves were sitting on the ground, all round a large hall; an old man with a white beard sat in the middle of the hall on a carpet, smoking a pipe, and he had before him a number of account-books and pens and ink. To him, the gipsy woman brought the princess, and after whispering a few words to him, she took the princess to one side of the hall, where were seated several little slave girls—some white and some black, under the care of a very cross-looking old woman, who grumbled a good deal about the princess bringing her parrot with her; but the gipsy woman told her they were to be sold together, and promising to come for her in the evening if she was not sold, she left her in charge of the old woman.

The little princess felt both fear and sorrow at being left

in the hands of strangers, and she sat on the ground amongst the other slave children as much out of sight as she could; she hugged her parrot in her arms, and kept her hidden in the bosom of her little gown, for fear she should be taken from her. Several persons who came to buy slaves looked at her, and asked her price of the old man who managed the sales, but the price he mentioned was too high for them. At last, a lady with a very forbidding countenance came by, and after looking at her, went to the old man to ask her price. The old woman who had charge of her, on seeing this, said, "I hope that lady will not buy you, for she is the worst mistress, and the most cruel woman in all the city. It is only last week that she drove a poor little negro slave girl to such desperation, by her ill usage, that in trying to escape over the walls of the court of her house, she fell to the ground and was killed."

"Oh," said the little princess, "pray do not let me be sold to her."

"I will not," said the old woman, "if I can help it: but the old man can sell you if he pleases."

"At least," said the princess, "do not let me be sold without the gipsy woman knowing; for I saved her life, and the lives of all her family, and I am sure she will not let that horrid woman have me."

Now the parrot heard all this, and putting her head out from under the princess's gown, she whispered in her ear, "I will go and fetch the gipsy woman"; and she flew straight out at the door of the bazaar and from thence over the houses, till she came to the gate where they had entered the city; a little way outside of this gate she found the gipsies encamped, and flying to the gipsy woman, she alighted on the ground at her feet, and taking the hem of her gown in her bill, gave a pull at it, and then began to shuffle along the ground towards the gate, chattering and making all sorts of signs with her head that the gipsy

should follow her. The gipsy saw what she wanted, and followed her towards the city gate, and the parrot kept flying before her and then perching till she brought her all the way to the gate of the bazaar.

Just as they got there they met the ill-looking lady coming out, holding the princess by the arm, who was crying bitterly; and there was a crowd of people about the gate of the bazaar, crying shame on the lady, and calling her a murderess and all sorts of names, and saying it was a shame she should have the little girl, for she would kill her as she had so many other slaves. As soon as the princess saw the gipsy woman she made a sudden spring, and escaping from the grasp of the ill-looking lady, she threw herself into the arms of the gipsy, and begged her not to let her be sold to that dreadful woman. The gipsy was moved, and assured the princess she should not be sold to her; but the ill-looking lady said: "She is sold to me already; I have paid for her, and here is the receipt." And she drew a bit of paper from her bosom, and held it up in her hand, when the parrot, flying suddenly over the heads of the crowd, snatched the paper from her hand, and flew away with it out of sight, and hid it at the top of a mosque close by the bazaar, and then flying back again, perched quietly on the top of the gate of the bazaar, where she could see all that took place.

By this time the disturbance was so great that the cadi, or judge, who lived near at hand, heard of it, and came to the bazaar with all his men to see what was the matter, and to keep the peace. Some cried one thing, and some another; the ill-looking lady declared she had bought the little girl, and the gipsy woman declared she had not sold her, and the people cried out it was a shame to let that vile murderess have her. The cadi ordered them all to be brought before him, and said to the ill-looking lady, "If you have bought the little girl, show me the receipt." She declared that the receipt had been snatched out of her hand by a parrot, and carried away.

"I don't believe that," said the cadi, "and unless you produce the receipt, I shall give up the little girl to the gipsy woman."

It was in vain that the ill-looking lady repeated what she had said; those who had not seen the parrot declared it was not true; and those who had, would not say anything about it, so the princess was restored to the gipsy woman, and the ill-looking lady went away looking worse and more dreadful than ever, for she had lost her victim and her money too.

The judgment of the cadi was given in the street, under the windows of his own house; and the princess was no sooner delivered to the gipsy, than a black slave came to her, and told her the cadi's wife wanted to speak to her;

she followed the slave, leading the princess by the hand into the cadi's house, and they were brought to the cadi's wife, who was sitting in a room with a balcony over the door of the house, with her little daughter by her side, who was about the same age as the princess, and who, having seen what had passed in the street, and being much taken with the appearance of the princess, had begged her mother to buy her. This was soon managed; the cadi's wife offered the gipsy woman a handsome price, and the princess was so much pleased with the looks of the cadi's little daughter, and of her mother, that she begged the gipsy woman to sell her to them, which was accordingly done; and the gipsy departed with her money, taking leave of the princess, and telling her she was in good hands and would lead a happy life.

After she was gone, the two little girls came into the balcony to look at the departing crowd, and the parrot, which was watching all that took place from her perch over the gate of the bazaar, soon perceived her little mistress in the balcony, and flying to her, perched on her shoulder. The cadi's daughter was much surprised, but the princess soon explained to her all about the parrot, and begged to be allowed to keep her, which was immediately granted.

The two little girls became much attached to each other, and led a very happy life together, learning the same lessons, and playing and taking their meals together, and sleeping in the same room; for though the princess was really the slave of the cadi's daughter, she was treated just as if she had been her sister; and before many days the princess had told her all her story, and had even let her into the secret of the magic ring.

CHAPTER VIII

One evening, after supper, the parrot said to the princess, "My dear, I think we had better let your grandfather know where you are; he must be very anxious about you, and to-morrow morning I will send the two daws, who roost every night on the minaret of the neighbouring mosque, to give him intelligence of what has happened to you, and to learn what are his wishes concerning you."

The princess gave her consent, and early the next morning she wrote a letter to her grandfather, and gave it to the parrot, who carried it to the daws, and desired them to lose no time in taking it to the old hermit at the source of the Ganges, and in bringing back an answer.

The old hermit had begun to be very uneasy about his grand-daughter, when one evening the two daws made their appearance with the princess's letter; and the old hermit, after having read it, wrote an answer, and delivered it to the daws, who, having stayed one day at the hermitage, to rest from their journey, flew back again to Lahore, and carried the hermit's letter straight to the apartment of the two little girls.

This was the Hermit's letter:

"To my dear Grandchild, whom I have never seen, but whom I love for her poor mother's sake,—I am rejoiced to hear that after so many troubles and dangers, you are happy and in good hands. Perhaps the best thing for you is that you should remain where you are with your young friend; but if anything happens to prevent this, and you are again in want of counsel or assistance, beyond what your faithful parrot can give you, do not forget to send again to your affectionate grandfather."

The two little girls continued to live very happily together, and became more and more attached to each other. The cadi and his wife were made acquainted with the princess's rank, and treated her with the greatest kindness and respect; but they told the two little girls to keep all the circumstances a close secret, for fear the wicked queen of Cashmere should hear of her and renew her persecutions; and it was agreed that she should continue to go by her slave name Shereen.

One day, as they were sitting at their work in the room of the mother of Zuleika (for that was the name of the princess's friend), the cadi came home from attending the king's court, and looked very grave and melancholy. His wife asked him what was the matter, and he said there was very bad news from Cashmere. It was reported that the king had suddenly died, and that the queen had proclaimed her little boy king, and had declared herself regent in his name. The little princess was very much shocked and grieved to hear of her father's death, and ran out of the room to conceal her trouble, and Zuleika followed to console her.

A few days afterwards, as the cadi's wife and the two little girls were sitting at the window, they saw a great crowd coming along the street, and when it came near, they perceived a grand procession of men in splendid dresses, with horses and camels, and in the midst of them, on a camel covered with embroidery, rode the ugly negro, Baboof, all over jewels and finery, and carrying in his hand a letter, wrapped in cloth of gold. The princess was much alarmed at the sight of him, and hid herself till the procession had passed. When the cadi came home from court, he looked graver and sadder than before; and being asked by his wife what the procession was, he told her it was an embassy from the queen of Cashmere, who had sent a most insolent letter to the king of Lahore, claiming tribute from him, and, in case of refusal, threatening war. He said, likewise, that the king was very angry, and had torn the queen's letter, and thrown it on the ground, and had ordered the embassy to depart, and that preparations were being made on every side for war.

The cadi's wife often sat with the two little girls at the window, watching the troops marching through the streets to join the army; and the parrot was generally of the party, for though she was not so young as she had been, she was very fond of looking at the soldiers, and would ruffle up her feathers, and scream with delight at the noise of the drums and cymbals.

One day, long after the departure of the last of the troops, as they sat looking up the empty street, the parrot said, in a melancholy voice, "I wish we could have some news of those charming warriors who are gone to fight in

our defence." Then, suddenly brightening up, she cried, "How foolish of me to forget the daws! they will bring us news without fail"; and away she flew to find the daws, and sent them off to follow the army, and bring back news of the war.

On the third evening after this, the two daws flew in at the window, worn out with fatigue and alarm; as soon as they had taken a little food and water which the princess

gave them, they told her that they had witnessed a great battle between the two armies, that the king of Lahore had been completely defeated, and his army dispersed, and that the army of the queen was in full march for Lahore, and would arrive the next day. The princess repeated all this to the cadi's wife, who was in the greatest grief and alarm, and who sent for her husband from the court, and told him what she had heard, and that it was by magic that she was acquainted with it, but she could not tell him more.

At first he disbelieved her and thought she had dreamt it, but seeing how alarmed she was, and knowing that she was a wise and good woman, he was convinced at last, and immediately went out to consult with the king's council what was best to be done. He did not come home till late at night, when he told his wife that the council had resolved, if the news were true, to submit to the queen's army in order to save the city from destruction. The cadi's wife immediately went to the princess, and said to her—"The queen's army will be in possession of the city to-morrow. It will not be safe for you to remain here—we must send you away to some place of safety."

While the cadi's wife was talking to the princess—who was weeping with fear and with grief at having again to quit such kind friends—the cadi was hastily summoned to attend the king, who had escaped from the battle, and who was holding a council to consider of the terms of peace which were offered by the enemy. The council was a very short one, and the cadi soon returned, and told them that the enemy would grant them peace, and spare the city, on payment of tribute and a very heavy ransom. Indeed, the sum demanded was so great, that it could only be raised by a general contribution of all the gold, silver, jewels, and other valuables, including horses and slaves, to be found in the city.

"We shall be reduced to poverty," said the cadi, "but we shall save our lives, and the enemy will leave the city in peace."

"Oh, then, Shereen need not be sent away," cried Zuleika, "for she will be quite safe here."

The cadi looked very sorrowful, and shook his head, and said that all the neighbours knew that his wife had bought Shereen for a slave at a high price, and she would be one of the first to be demanded in payment of the ransom; that the house would be searched, as well as every other house in the city, for valuables that might be concealed, so that they could not hide her in the house; and that there was no place of safety to send her to out of the city, which was surrounded by the enemy's soldiers.

Having said this, the cadi went out, leaving them all in greater grief than before. But the old parrot, who had listened to all that passed, stepped down from her perch on to the princess's shoulder, and kissing her, bid her not cry, for she knew a safe place to hide her in. The two daws, she said, lived in a ruined mosque, near the back of the garden. This mosque had only one minaret left, at the top of which was a little chamber, where she would be quite safe; but of the stairs which led to it, the lower half had fallen down, and the only way to get up into it would be by a ladder.

"If our friends," said the parrot, "will make a ladder of some of the silken cords of which I see plenty amongst the furniture of this place, the two daws will fly with it to the top of the minaret, and I can fasten one end to the bottom of the remaining stairs, and let the other end down to you; but the ladder must be made as light as possible, or the daws will not be able to carry it."

The princess repeated all this to the cadi's wife, and all three immediately set to work to make the rope ladder. The parrot took a little ball of twine in her claws, and flew up to the lowest of the remaining stairs of the minaret, and letting the ball fall down, while she held the end of the twine above, it unrolled as it fell. She then flew down after it, and picking it up, flew with it to the princess, and showed her how much was unrolled, and that gave them the length necessary for the rope ladder. Zuleika sat in the window looking down the street, to give notice if the officers of the king should make their appearance to search the house; but they had many houses to search first, and by the time it grew dusk in the evening, the cadi's wife and the princess had made a ladder of silk-cord, long enough and sufficiently strong to bear the princess's weight.

CHAPTER IX

As soon as it was dark, the cadi's wife and the two little girls went with the parrot secretly into the garden, and to a terrace overlooking the ground in which the ruined mosque stood, which was very near the garden wall. They found a ladder in the garden, by which they reached the ground outside —the parrot having previously ascertained from the daws, who were on the watch, that all was safe. As soon as they were under the minaret, the princess gave the rope ladder which she had wrapped round a small stick, to the two daws, and told them to fly up with it. Each of them took one end of the stick in its claws, and tried to fly up; but, though the silk-cord was so fine that the ladder made a very small bundle, it was too heavy for the poor birds, and they came fluttering to the ground with it. The parrot tried to help them, but she was such a clumsy flier, that she only got in their way, and made matters worse.

They were all in despair, and were just going to return

to the garden, when they heard a frightful shriek just over their heads, and on looking up, they could see, against the faint light of the sky, a large bird fly to the top of the ruin, and perch there. It was an enormous owl.

"The talisman! the talisman!" cried the parrot—"give me the talisman!" and snatching the ring from the princess, she flew up and touched the owl with it, to his great astonishment. The old parrot then, with a most important voice, ordered the owl to take the rope ladder and carry it up to the top of the minaret, which he did, and then, bowing his great horned head to the parrot, asked if there were any more commands for him.

"None," said the parrot, "except to keep watch in this ruin at night, and give notice if any danger approaches"; and so the owl was dismissed.

The parrot then managed to carry the rope ladder down the remaining stairs, and twisted one end of it firmly round an old nail in the wall of the staircase, and let the other end fall down to the ground. The princess and her two friends were standing below, and, having taken leave of each other with many kisses and tears, she began to climb the ladder; and as soon as she was safe at the top, she pulled it up after her, and her friends returned to the house, leaving the princess with her three birds in her new retreat. She could not see what sort of a place it was, but wrapped herself up in a cloak she had brought, and soon fell fast asleep.

The princess was awakened by the sun shining in through a doorway in the wall, and found herself in a very little round chamber, which communicated with the gallery outside by means of the doorway; and on one side, in the stone floor, was an opening communicating with the stairs, and through which she had come up. She was afraid to go out into the gallery, for fear of being seen—for the cadi's wife and the parrot had charged her on no account to run any risk of being seen. The daws were gone in search of food, and the parrot, as soon as she and the princess had breakfasted on some provisions she had brought with her, flew down into the garden to hear how things were going on.

She found the place in a great commotion. The king's officers were in the house, searching for valuables. The cadi produced all his gold, silver, and jewels, and whatever else

was of value. His horses were brought from the stables, and all the slaves were mustered in the court, that the officers might choose those that were worth seizing. Having chosen such as they thought worth taking, they were going away, when a slave-girl, who was amongst those that were taken, cried out to the officers—"There is another slave-girl somewhere in the house, who is worth more than all of us put together; but she is the favourite, and they have hid her."

The officers asked what her name was. "We call her the parrot girl," said she, "because she always has a nasty old parrot with her: there it is," said she, pointing to the parrot, "and you may be sure the parrot girl is not far off."

It was jealousy that made the slave girl so spiteful. The cadi said to the officers, "I have such a slave, but where she is I do not know; my house is open to you, search everywhere."

It was true he did not know where she was; all his wife had told him was that the princess had gone to a safe place, and he did not wish to hear more, that he might be clear of blame. The officers searched everywhere in vain; at last they said they supposed she had run away, and would probably be caught before long; so taking their spoil with them they departed, leaving the house stripped of all its most valuable furniture, and with only a few old slaves not worth taking away. As soon as they were gone, Zuleika ran to her mother, and said, "Oh mamma! Shereen may come back now!"

"No," said her mother, "she is much safer where she is; it will not be safe to bring her back till the enemy's army is gone."

Zuleika was very sorry to hear this, but she begged her mother to let her go and visit the princess at night, to which she at last consented, if there should be no appearance of danger.

"Oh!" said Zuleika, "those dear birds will watch, so that we cannot be surprised."

She then sent by the parrot a note to the princess, promising to come and see her as soon as it was dark, and to bring some provisions with her.

Nearly all day the princess sat in her little chamber, sometimes talking to the parrot, or working, and sometimes

The three birds were also a good deal occupied in bringing their mistress provisions from Zuleika, who was not allowed to repeat her visit for two or three days, for fear of discovery. Her next visit to the minaret was late at night, because she had to wait till the moon was gone down, and she and the princess had so much to say to one another that it was almost morning before they parted, and the princess was so sleepy that she forgot to draw up the rope-ladder again after Zuleika's departure.

The next morning, the parrot awoke before her, and having sent the daws off in search of intelligence to the Cashmerian camp, she herself flew to the cadi's house to get her mistress's breakfast. The parrot had not been long away when the princess was awakened by a horrid laugh, which sounded close to her, and she was struck with terror when she saw coming up through the opening which led to the stairs, a head and shoulders. She knew the face too well; it was that of the spiteful slave-girl, who had attempted to betray her to the officers when they searched the cadi's house, and who had always been her enemy.

"Ha, ha! my fine parrot-girl," cried she, "I have found you out, have I? I will soon deliver you to those that will be glad to get you, and who will give me a good reward, too!" She then sprang into the chamber, and before the princess had recovered from her amazement, she seized her and bound her hand and foot with her own scarf, which she tore in two for the purpose, and then saying, "I think you will hardly be able to escape again before I return," she went down the rope-ladder, and as soon as she reached the ground, with a violent jerk she pulled it from the nail to which it was fastened above, and down it fell through the trap door. The spiteful slave gathered up the rope-ladder, and carried it away with her in great haste, leaving the princess lying helpless at the top of the minaret, and without any means of getting down to escape, even if she had not been bound hand and foot. How the slave-girl came to discover her was thus:—She herself had managed to escape that very night from the building in which the slaves who had been seized to make up the ransom, were kept, and had found her way to the ruined mosque, in hopes of being able to conceal herself there. Finding the rope-ladder hanging down inside the minaret, she climbed up to see where it led to, and finding the princess asleep, it immediately came into her head to betray her to the king's officers, for she not only hated her out of jealousy, but she knew that a reward was offered for all runaway slaves, and that if she delivered up so valuable a slave as the princess, she should not only be forgiven herself for running away, but probably be set at liberty besides by way of reward.

The slave-girl never stopped till she came to the building where her fellow slaves were confined, and going straight to the gate, she desired the porter to take her to the keeper of the slaves. When she appeared before him, he began to threaten her with punishment for running away, but she interrupted him and said, "What will you give me if I find you a runaway slave worth one hundred pieces of gold?"

"If you can do that," said the keeper, "you shall be set free yourself, and have five pieces of gold; but if you deceive me you shall be beaten on the soles of your feet till you can neither walk nor stand."

"I consent," said the girl, "but there is no time to be lost; come with me, and bring a ladder with you as long as this rope-ladder which you see, and I will deliver into your hands the favourite slave of the cadi's wife, who is well worth the money I mentioned."

The keeper immediately sent two or three soldiers with a ladder to accompany the girl, who brought them straight to the foot of the minaret. The ladder was then raised, and one of the soldiers went up, but he found the chamber empty, and no traces of the princess except a few articles of furniture with which Zuleika had supplied her, and the fragments of her scarf, which appeared all torn to pieces, and stained with blood in several places. This the man brought down with him, and after searching all the ruins in vain, they returned to the keeper of the slaves, who was greatly enraged, and ordered the spiteful slave to be beaten on the soles of her feet for deceiving him; but she cried out that she had not deceived him, and said that if the cadi's house was searched again, the parrot-girl would be sure to be found, as she could not have had time to go far, and would certainly take refuge there in whatever manner she had escaped.

While this was going on, the king himself came to the slave prison, to see how many had been collected, and asking what was the matter, the keeper told him all that had happened. The king was very angry when he heard that the cadi's slave had been concealed, and swore that unless she was found his own daughter Zuleika should be seized in her place; and he immediately sent an officer of his guard and a number of soldiers to search for the princess, and if they could not find her they were ordered to seize Zuleika instead. Accordingly, they went at once to the cadi's house, and searched it and the gardens thoroughly, but no princess could they find. Zuleika and her mother were much alarmed, fearing that the princess's retreat in the minaret might be discovered; but they soon found out, from what the officer said, that it had been searched already without finding her; and though this relieved their fears in some degree, they were greatly troubled to think what could have become of her, especially when he showed them the bloody pieces of her scarf. But what was their dismay when the officer declared he had orders to seize Zuleika, and take her away as a slave; and in spite of the cries and tears of both mother and daughter, she was carried off to the slave prison! As she passed through the court-yard to her cell, she saw the spiteful slave-girl led away by two of the attendants to receive the punishment her wickedness so richly deserved, though she was unjustly sentenced to it by the keeper of the slaves.

CHAPTER XI

How it came to pass that the princess was not found in the minaret where she had been left bound hand and foot was thus. As she lay helpless on the floor she saw a pair of great staring eyes looking at her through the hole in the wall, through which she used to watch Zuleika's window. At first she was frightened, but in a moment she perceived it was the great owl, who was perched amongst some ivy outside, and was looking through the hole. She immediately bethought herself of the talisman, and managed to lift her fastened hands up so as to present the ring to the sight of the owl, and cried out, "Oh, owl! owl! help me for the sake of this!" The owl no sooner saw the talisman and heard these words, than he came to the princess and asked what were her commands.

"Unbind my hands and feet," said she, "if you can."

The owl could not untie the pieces of scarf that bound her: but with his strong, hooked bill and sharp claws he tore them off, and in so doing he could not help slightly wounding the princess, which caused the stains of blood on the pieces of scarf found by the soldier who climbed up in search of her. No sooner was she free, than she looked round for some means of escape, but there was none (the ladder being gone) unless she could jump down to the ground, and the minaret was much too high for her to venture so desperate a leap.

"Oh, owl! owl!" cried she again, "cannot you help me to get down from this place, before my cruel enemy returns?"

The owl was one of that sort almost as large as an eagle, but of course he was not strong enough to support the weight of the princess in the air, or he would have carried her down to the ground, so he replied, "Wait a moment, fair princess, and I will call my wife, who is taking her morning's sleep amongst the ruins close by, and I think we two together can give you support enough with our wings to bring you safely to the ground."

Then going out to the balcony he screeched in his shrillest tones to his wife to come and help him, till all the ruins echoed: and presently a great female owl came flitting to the balcony, and said, "What is the matter, my lord? why have you awakened me at this time of day?"

The he-owl then answered by pointing with his bill to the talisman on the princess's finger, who had followed him to the balcony, and addressing her said, "There is no time to be lost. Take firm hold of my legs with one hand, and of my wife's legs with the other, and throw yourself boldly from the balcony upon that leafy bush below; we can support you with our wings enough to break your fall."

No sooner said than done. The princess grasped the legs of the friendly owls, and threw herself from the balcony; down they went all three with a tremendous rushing of wings, and the princess fell on the springy branches of the bush without receiving any hurt at all, and letting go the legs of the owls they flew up again to the ruin, while she scrambled through the branches to the ground.

As soon as she was clear of the bush, she looked about to see which way she had better go to escape the danger of pursuit, when she caught sight of the soldiers, who were just coming towards the ruin to take her. Fortunately, they could not see her; and she immediately darted away on the opposite side to that by which they were coming, and keeping out of sight, she ran with all her speed towards a little winding lane which she saw before her, with garden walls on each side of it. She had run some way up this lane, when just as she came near a door in the left-hand wall, it was slowly and cautiously opened, and she had but just time to hide herself behind a fig-tree which grew out of the wall, when she saw a woman slave come out of the door, and after looking up and down the lane, walk rapidly up it. As soon as she was out of sight, the princess came from behind the fig-tree, and as she passed the door, seeing that it was not quite shut, she pushed it cautiously open and peeped in, and seeing that within was a large garden, closely planted, and that nobody was in sight, she thought she should be safer if she could hide herself there for the present, than if she went she knew not where up the lane. So she went into the garden, and, leaving the door as she found it, she hastened to conceal herself in the nearest clump of trees.

She had hardly done so, when she heard the door shut, and peeping out, she saw the same slave, who had just returned, bolt the door and proceed towards the house, of which she could see the roof at the other end of the garden. She now felt herself comparatively safe; but to be safer still, she climbed up into a large cypress-tree, the thick foliage of which completely concealed her, and there she determined to wait till night, and then to endeavour to reach the cadi's house, where she was sure Zuleika and her mother would give her protection if they could. Indeed, she had nowhere else to go to.

Long and weary was the day, but night came at last. The princess did not, however, venture from her hiding-place till past the middle of the night, when she thought she should be less likely to meet anybody on her way to the cadi's house. She then came down from the tree, and unbolting the garden door, she went into the lane, and returning by the way that she had come in the morning, she soon found herself in the open ground surrounding the ruined mosque. She made her way, as well as she could guess in the darkness, towards the cadi's garden, hoping to find some means of climbing over the wall, and so getting in without being observed by any of the slaves; but just as she was passing the ruined mosque, she saw her friends, the owls, come flying over her head in the faint starlight. She called out to them, and asked whether they had seen anything of the parrot or the two daws. "Yes," said the owl, perching on a wall, "they are all three roosting here in the ruin, and have been flying about all day looking for you."

"Oh, bring me to them!" said the princess; and the owl, flying into the ruin, soon reappeared with the parrot fluttering after him. The parrot flew into the princess's bosom with an hysterical scream, and said, "Oh, my dear child, have I found you at last? I feared some terrible misfortune had happened to you."

The princess then told her how she had escaped, and that she was going to try to get into the cadi's garden, but the parrot interrupted her, and told her of poor Zuleika's being seized for a slave instead of her. She was overwhelmed with grief at hearing this, and declared that she would go and give herself up to save Zuleika; and in spite of all the parrot could say, she instantly set out to fulfil her determination, for she could not bear to think that she had brought such a calamity on Zuleika and her mother.

"Well, my dear child," said the parrot, "if you are bent on destroying yourself, at least, I will go with you; but first I will tell the daws to remain about this ruin, that, in case of need, we may know where to find them."

Having done this, the parrot nestled under the princess's cloak, and she left the ruin, and going into the nearest street, went straight to the door of the cadi's house and knocked loudly. After some time, an old slave put his head out of the window, and asked who was there.

"It is I, Shereen," said the princess, "let me in."

The old slave opened the door, and by the princess's desire, took her to the women's apartment. She was admitted by Zuleika's nurse, who, as soon as she saw her, began to lament Zuleika's misfortune, and to tell her what had happened; but the princess stopped her, and said, "I know it all, but she shall not suffer for me: I am come to give myself up." She then desired the nurse to take her to

Zuleika's mother; and this was done, when the princess, throwing herself into the arms of the cadi's wife, told her she was come to give herself up, and save her friend. The cadi's wife kissed her, and wept over her, but did not oppose her design, for she knew it was the only way by which her daughter could be restored to her.

But now the poor princess, not having eaten all day, and being quite exhausted with all she had undergone, fell in a swoon on the floor. The cadi's wife had her put to bed, and as soon as she came to herself, she begged for a little food, which was given to her; and she then fell asleep and did not awaken till broad daylight. As soon

as she had breakfasted, the cadi's wife took her to her husband, who was informed of her noble behaviour, which he praised very highly; and after taking a mournful and pathetic leave of the cadi's wife, he led her away by the hand, and took her to the slave-prison. They were immediately taken to the keeper, to whom the cadi was relating the object of his visit, when they were interrupted by the arrival of the vizier, who had come to inspect the slaves. The keeper referred the cadi to the vizier, who, when he had heard what he had to say—being no friend of his—declared that it was impossible to let Zuleika go, for there was so much difficulty in raising the ransom for the city, that the king had given him orders to seize and make slaves of any one he could lay his hands on, so that both Zuleika and Shereen must be kept.

It was in vain that the cadi intreated, and threatened, and tore his beard with rage and grief. He went straight to the palace, and complained to the king that his daughter had been seized as a slave; but the king said there was no help for it, the money must be raised, and that he would sell the cadi himself if any person would buy him.

CHAPTER XII

The only comfort the two little girls had in their misfortune was, that they were confined together in the same cell. It was a very small one, with a little window in it just large enough for the parrot to go through. Through this window the parrot went to learn the news in the city, and to carry a note from Zuleika to her mother. When she came back, she told the princess that the cadi could not raise money enough to redeem Zuleika, and that in a day or two all the slaves would be taken to the Cashmerian camp, and that the enemy's army would then immediately march back to Cashmere, with all their spoil; so that there was the greatest danger of the princess falling again into the hands of her greatest enemy.

"There is but one hope," said the parrot: "give me your ring, and I will send the daws with it to your grandfather; they will tell him all that has happened, and he is so wise that he will know how to help us if any help is possible;

but he can do nothing for us without the ring, for that gives command over all the birds of the air, and it was with this ring that the famous enchanter, Moozuffer, ruled over the birds, and by their help worked so many wonders." The princess gave the ring to the parrot, and she immediately flew with it to the ruin, and calling the daws, ordered one of them to fly with all speed to the hermitage at the source of the Ganges, and to give the hermit the ring, and tell him all that had happened. She told the other daw to keep in the neighbourhood of the camp, and to fly after the army whenever it marched. Having given these instructions to the daws, she returned to the slave-prison.

Next morning the slaves were taken to the camp, and delivered to the Cashmerian general, and the army immediately marched on its return to Cashmere. The two little girls were carried together in a close litter, and the parrot with them, but for want of the ring the poor bird and her mistress were no longer able to converse together, which was a great grief to them.

In this way they travelled many days, till at length they arrived within a day's journey of Cashmere. Here the army halted in a great plain, and the queen came from the city, with all her court, to receive her victorious army, and to see the spoils of war they had brought with them. The army was all drawn up in grand array, and the treasures, the gold, silver, and jewels, rich silks and shawls, beautiful horses, and the slaves which had been brought from Lahore, were placed in front of the general's tent, where they formed a splendid spectacle. The queen sat in her howdah on an elephant most gorgeously caparisoned, and rode in front of the long lines of soldiers, attended by the general and all her court. When she came opposite the place where the

and kissed her; and was going to take her with him on one of the elephants, when she begged him to let Zuleika come with them. This was granted; and the old king, with the

princess, and Zuleika, proceeded at the head of the army to take possession of his ancient capital.

You may be sure that the parrot was not left behind, but sat proudly on the princess's arm, bowing graciously to the shouting people in the streets; while the two daws flew joyously overhead, to resume their old roosting-place in the palace garden; and the flock of eagles, released from their service, flew back to their home in the mountains.

The first thing the princess did after her arrival at the palace was to beg her grandfather to send to Lahore, for Zuleika's father and mother, who came with joy to rejoin their daughter, and had a house given them close to the royal palace, so that the two little girls saw each other every day, and passed most of their time together. Neither did the princess forget her old friend, the fisherman, who, at her request, was appointed by the old king captain of the royal pleasure-boats.